_____

Your Name Here

Birthday
☆ Star of the week ☆
Children's Day ◎ Hospital Stay
Off to Camp ♡ Valentine's Day ♡
First day of school ☺ Moving
♡ Grandparent's Day ♡
🌷 Sweetest Day 🌸
Just Because...

Or any other day to
celebrate your love for a child

Your special occasion:

3 Children's Stories of Love

Love, by Trio

to Jo-Ann,
here's to a
joyful,
fun &
wonderful
Monday morning
with the kids!

joyful reading♡
Darcy Anderson
Hill

Darcy Hill.

Look an 1, 2

nd see

, 3 ...

Story
3

What Color Do You Paint Love?

Dedication

Dedicated with love
to children of all ages
who share a common
playground known as
IMAGINATION.

Published by
by TRIO™
Box 878
Green Bay, Wisconsin 54305

Text copyright © 2001 by Darcy Anderson Hill
Illustrations copyright © 2001 by Sasha Kinens

 Visit us on the web!
www.bytriochildrensbooks.com

Library of Congress Cataloging-in-Publication Data
(Provided by Quality Books, Inc.)

Hill, Darcy Anderson.
    Love, by TRIO / by Darcy Anderson Hill ; illustrated
by Sasha Kinens. -- 1st ed.
    p. cm.
    LCCN 2001091356
    SUMMARY : Fun and melodic exploration of love as seen
through a child's eyes.
    Audience: Ages 4 - 7.
    ISBN 0-9710840-0-9

    1. Love -- Juvenile literature. 2. Wonder -- Juvenile
literature. 3. Values -- Juvenile literature.
    4. Children's songs. [1. Love. 2. Wonder. 3. Values.
    4. Songs. 5. Stories in rhyme.] I. Title. II. Kinens, Sasha.

PZ8.3.H53Lov 2001   [E]
                        QBI01 - 700689

Watercolors were used for full-color illustrations
Printed in the United States of America
Produced by Redman Productions Inc., Redwood Falls, Minnesota
Logo Design by F. Patrick LaSalle, Design/Graphics, Rockford, Illinois

First Edition, First Printing 2001

L-O-V-E

 Story

1

L-O-V-E

Love is special
Keeps you warm
Just like the sun,

L-O-V-E

Love is special,

L-O-V-E

Love someone!

L-O-V-E

Hand to hand,

L-O-V-E

Knee to knee,

L-O-V-E

Foot to foot,

L-O-V-E

Hugs are free!

L-O-V-E

Love is perfect
Shares a smile
And brings the fun!

L-O-V-E

Love is perfect,

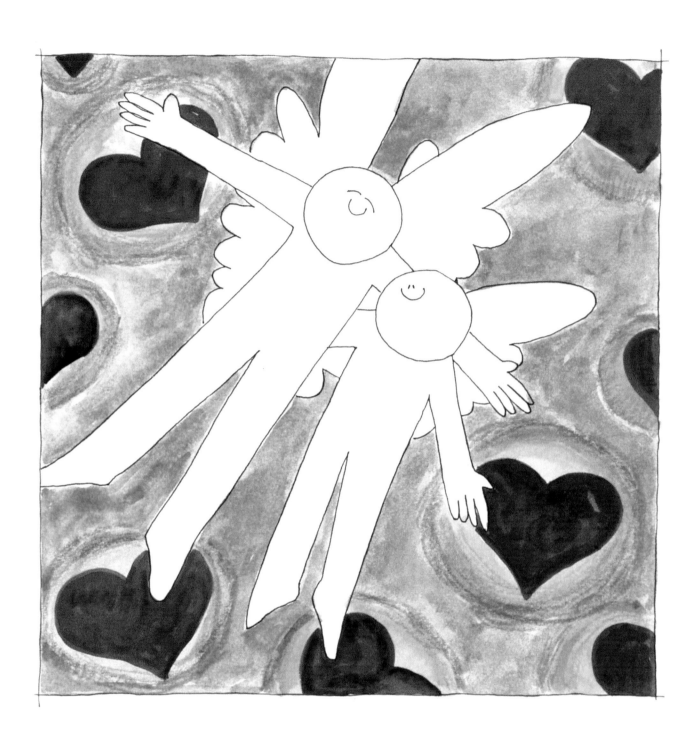

L-O-V-E

Love someone!

L-O-V-E

Reach for stars,

L-O-V-E

Jump with glee!

L-O-V-E

Make a wish,

L-O-V-E

Hugs are free!
Hugs are free!
You and me.

L-O-V-E

words and music by
Darcy Anderson Hill © 2001

Who Should I Send A Valentine To?

 Story

Who should I send
a Valentine to?

Would you mind if
I sent one to you?

Covered with hearts
and some pretty white lace,

would it put a smile
on your face?

Why do we need a holiday
to send out the love
that we feel?

Couldn't it just be any day
that Valentine love
could be real?

I know who I'll send
a Valentine to...

every day from my heart,
I'll send one to you!

Who Should I Send a Valentine To?

words and music by
Darcy Anderson Hill © 2001

What Color Do You Paint Love?

 Story **3**

What color do you paint love;
what shape and what size?

Do you give it
stripes and spots,

or arms and legs
and eyes?

What color do you
paint love?
Is it a box or a ball?

Do you paint it
just an inch,

or is it ten feet tall?

What color do you paint love?
Rainbows of paint
for a start...

brushes big and brushes small
painting with all of
your heart

What Color Do You Paint Love?

words and music by
Darcy Anderson Hill © 2001

1. What col - or do you pai - nt love?
2. What col - or do you pai - nt love?
3. What col - or do you pai - nt love?

What shape and what si - ze? Do you give i - t stripes
Is..it..a box or a ba - ll? Do you paint i - t just
rainbows..of paint for a sta - rt? Bru - shes big a - nd bru -

a - nd spots or arms and legs a - nd ey - es?
a - n inch or is it ten fe - et ta - ll?
sh - es small painting with all of your hea - rt.